St. Vincent's Catholic Primary
Orchard Road
Altrincham
Cheshire
WA15 8EY

First published in 1991 by
Simon & Schuster Young Books
Campus 400
Maylands Avenue
Hemel Hempstead
Herts, HP2 7EZ

Reprinted in 1991, 1992, 1993

Typeset in 20pt Avant Garde by
Goodfellow & Egan, Phototypesetters Ltd., Cambridge
Printed and Bound in Belgium by Proost International Book Production

British Library Cataloguing in Publication Data
Clark, Dorothy
  Grandpa's Handkerchief
  I. Title II, Dodds, Siobhan
  823.'914 (J)
ISBN 0-7500-0783-4
ISBN 0-7500-0784-2 pbk

GRANDPA'S HANDKERCHIEF

DOROTHY CLARK
ILLUSTRATED BY
SIOBHAN DODDS

SIMON & SCHUSTER
YOUNG BOOKS

On **Monday** Grandpa used his **yellow** handkerchief for . . .

waving to trains.

On **Tuesday** Grandpa used his **white** handkerchief for bandaging a knee.

On **Wednesday** Grandpa used his **pink** handkerchief for playing pirates.

On **Thursday** Grandpa used his **orange** handkerchief for reminding him about a birthday.

On **Friday** Grandpa used his **green** handkerchief for wiping away a crumb.

On **Saturday** Grandpa used his **red** handkerchief for cheering the team.

On **Sunday** Grandpa used his **blue** handkerchief for making a sun hat.

On sportsday Grandpa used his **brown** handkerchief for running in a three-legged race.

On holiday Grandpa used his **purple** handkerchief for making a sailing boat.

"Better than paper handkerchiefs
any day!" says Grandpa,
"Especially for . . .

AH-AH-AH-CHOO!

Monday

Tuesday

Wednesday

yellow

white

pink

brown

Thursday

Friday

Saturday

Sunday

orange

green

red

blue

purple